A Rudd's Rhyming Children's Book
Production 2020

© The World of Eggs 2021

All rights reserved. No part of this publication may be reproduced, stored in a retrieval system, or transmitted in any form or by any means, electronic, mechanical, photocopying, recording or otherwise, without prior written permission from the author.

Simon Rudd asserts the moral right to be identified as the author and illustrator of this work.

This book is dedicated to...

Oscar Leo Cooper

11th January 2021   9lb 12^{oz}

This book belongs to...

There are many different egg types,

Some are good and fly around in...

tights.

Some are bad,
nasty and mean.

Some are just rotten, smelly and green.

A cowboy egg you might think is strange, he's herding cow eggs on the range!

This one's on a wall but at a glance,

He's wearing nothing, only underpants.

There are Unicorn eggs that are full of...

grace,

There are even eggs from outer space.

Some can be heavy or light as a feather,

Some can be silly,

some can be clever.

Some go to work just for fun...

But dream of bathing in the sun.

Some eggs like to dream at night,

Of fearsome Dragons and daring Knights.

Some get scared and like to scream,

Especially on egg...

Halloween.

Some sledge down hills in a frying pan, before building a giant egg Snowman.

On the 25th of December you could see,

Father Eggmas next to your tree.

If I think and use my head to decide which is my favourite egg.

I pick chocolate ones my good friend,
So Happy Easter and the end.

Happy Easter.
The End.

Printed in Great Britain
by Amazon